The
Gigantic
Turnip

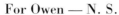

For Owen — N. S.

Barefoot Beginners
an imprint of
Barefoot Books
37 West 17th Street
4th Floor East
New York, New York 10011

Illustrations copyright © 1998 by Niamh Sharkey

The moral right of Niamh Sharkey to be identified as the illustrator
of this work has been asserted.

This book is printed on 100% acid-free paper

Graphic design by Tom Grzelinski, England
Colour reproduction by Grafiscan, Italy
Printed in Singapore by Tien Wah Press (Pte) Ltd

3 5 7 9 8 6 4 2

U.S. Cataloging-in-Publication Data / Library of Congress Standards

Tolstoy, Aleksei.
    The gigantic turnip / Aleksei Tolstoy and Niamh Sharkey.
[40] p. : col. ill. ; 28 cm.
Summary: A hilarious retelling of the famous Russian folktale of the turnip that
grows and grows and grows. Simple vocabulary, lots of repetition, and quirky
illustrations add to its overall appeal.
ISBN: 1-902283-12-0
1. Folklore -- Russia. I. Sharkey, Niamh.   II. Title.
398.2/ 0947 --dc21   1999 AC   CIP

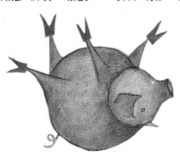
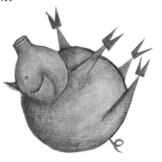

The Gigantic Turnip

Aleksei Tolstoy
&
Niamh Sharkey

BAREFOOT BOOKS

Long ago, an old man and an old woman lived together in a crooked old cottage with a large, overgrown garden.

The old man
and the old
woman

kept six yellow canaries,

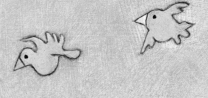

five white geese,

four speckled hens,

three black cats,

two pot-bellied pigs

and one big brown cow.

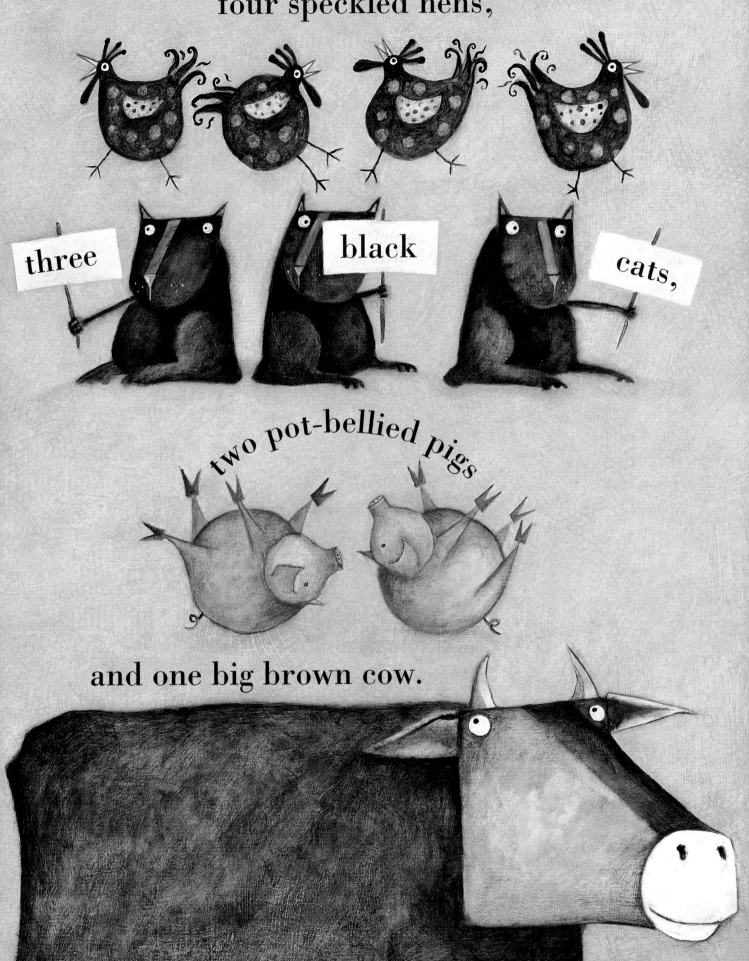

On a fine March morning, the
old woman sat up in bed, sniffed
the sweet spring air and said,
"It's time for us to sow the
vegetables!" So the old man
and the old woman went out
into the garden.

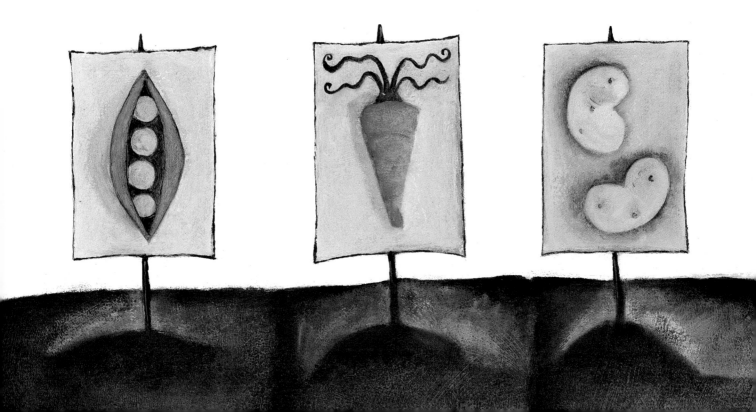

They sowed peas and carrots
and potatoes and beans. Last of
all, they sowed
turnips.

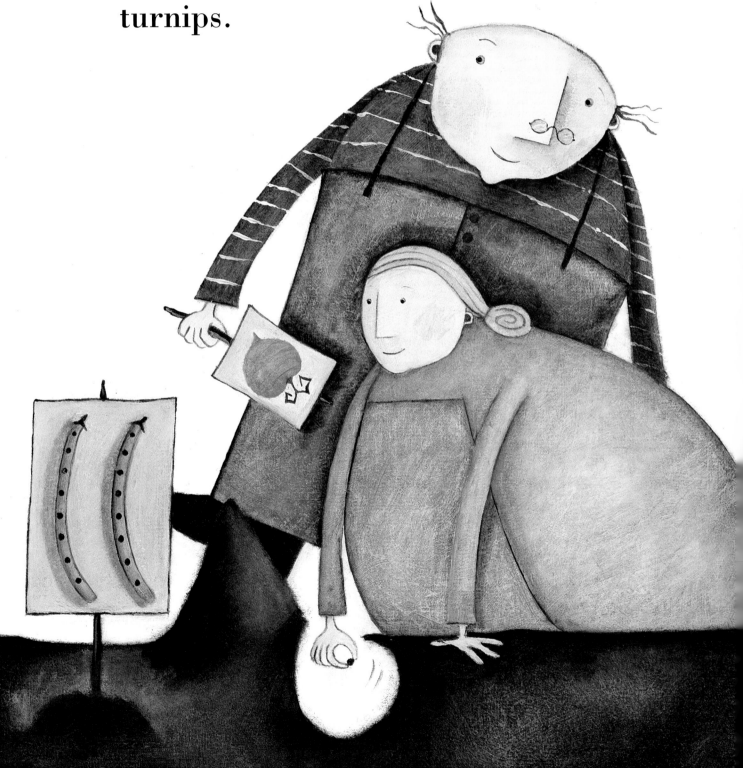

That night, rain fell — pitter, patter! — on the garden of the crooked old cottage. The old man and the old woman smiled as they slept.

The rain would help the seeds swell and produce fine juicy vegetables.

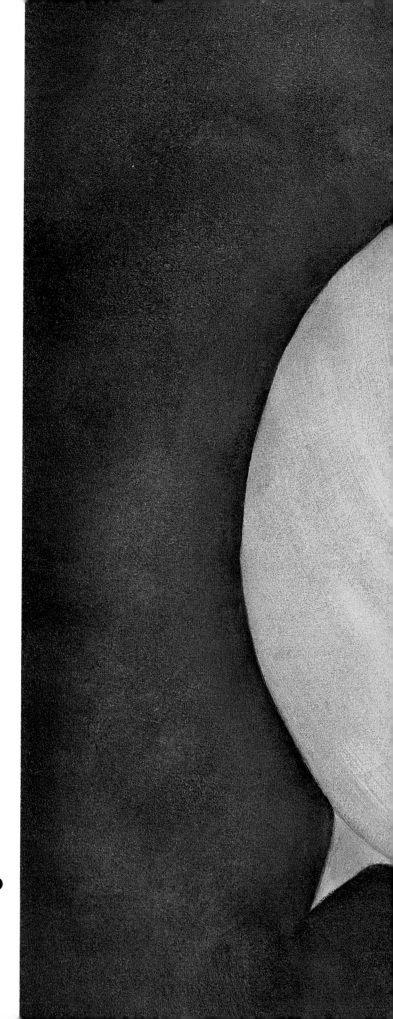

Spring passed
and the summer
sun ripened the
vegetables. The
old man and the
old woman
harvested their
carrots and
potatoes and
peas and beans
and turnips. At
the end of the
row, there was
just one turnip
left. It looked
very big.
In fact, it looked

gigantic.

On a fine
September
morning, the
old man sat up
in bed, sniffed
the cool fall air
and said,
"It's time for us to
pull up that turnip."

And out he went.

The old man pulled and
heaved and tugged and
yanked, but the turnip
would not move.

The old man went to find
the old woman.

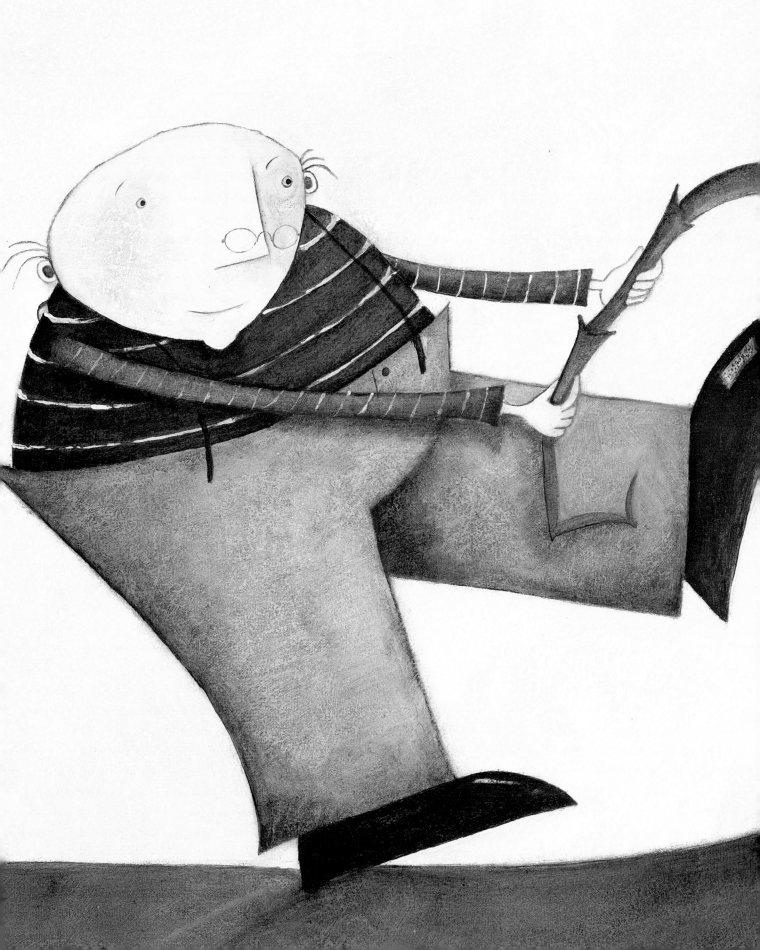

The old woman wrapped her arms round the old man's waist. Both of them pulled and heaved and tugged and yanked, but still the turnip would not move.

So the old woman went to fetch the big brown cow.

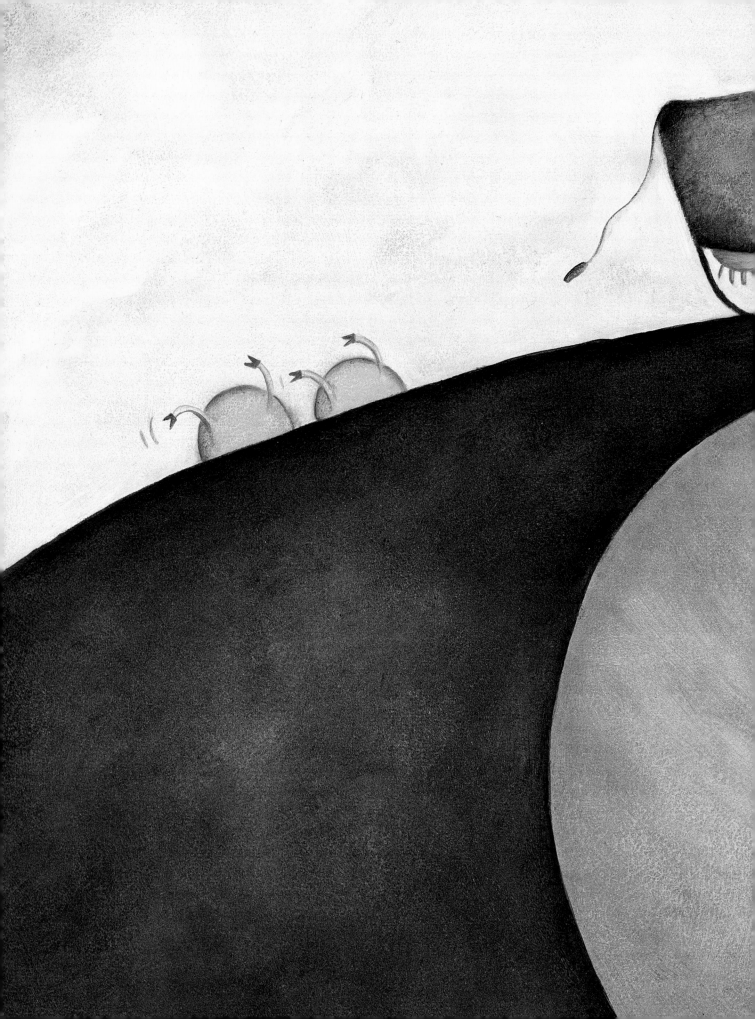

The old man, the old woman and the
big brown cow pulled and heaved
and tugged and yanked, but still the
turnip would not move.

So the old man mopped his brow and
went to fetch the two pot-bellied pigs.

The old man, the old woman, the big brown cow and the two pot-bellied pigs pulled and heaved and tugged and yanked. Still the turnip would not move.

So the old woman rolled up her sleeves and went to fetch the three black cats.

The old man, the old woman, the big brown cow, the two pot-bellied pigs and the three black cats pulled and heaved and tugged and yanked. Still the turnip would not move.

So one of the cats twitched her tail and went to fetch the four speckled hens.

The old man, the old
woman, the big brown
cow, the two pot-bellied
pigs, the three black cats
and the four speckled
hens pulled and heaved
and tugged and yanked.
Still the turnip would
not move.

So one of the hens shook
her feathers and went to
fetch the five white geese.

The old man, the old woman, the big brown cow, the two pot-bellied pigs, the three black cats, the four speckled hens and the five white geese pulled and heaved and tugged and yanked. Still the turnip would not move.

So one of the geese
craned her neck and
went to fetch the
six yellow canaries.

The old man, the old woman, the big brown cow, the two pot-bellied pigs, the three black cats, the four speckled hens,

the five white geese and the
six yellow canaries pulled
and heaved and tugged
and yanked.

Still the turnip would not move.

The old man scratched his head.

The animals and birds lay
on the ground gasping.

The old woman had an idea.

The old woman went into the kitchen and put a piece of cheese by the mousehole. Soon a hungry little mouse popped its head out of the hole. The old woman caught the mouse and carried it outside.

The old man, the old woman, the big brown cow, the two pot-bellied pigs, the three black cats, the four speckled hens,

the five white geese, the
six yellow canaries and the
hungry little mouse pulled
and heaved and tugged
and yanked.

Pop!

The gigantic turnip came flying out of the ground and everyone fell over. The canaries fell on the mouse, the geese fell on the canaries, the hens fell on the geese, the cats fell on the hens, the pigs fell on the cats, the cow fell on the pigs, the old woman fell on the cow and the old man fell on the old woman.

All of them lay on the ground and laughed.

That night the old man and
the old woman made a huge
bowl of turnip stew.
Everyone ate as much as
they could. And do you know
what? The hungry little
mouse ate the most of all.

BAREFOOT BOOKS publishes high-quality picture books for
children of all ages and specializes in the work of artists and writers from
many cultures. If you have enjoyed this book and would like to receive a copy of
our current catalog, please contact our New York office —
Barefoot Books Inc., 37 West 17th Street, 4th Floor East, New York, New York 10011
e-mail: ussales@barefoot-books.com   website: www.barefoot-books.com